Finally! An Unexpected Love Story

Finally! An Unexpected Love Story

Finally! An Unexpected Love Story

L. E. HEWITT AND SUZANNE PUREWAL

Purewal Publishing, LLC
Noblesville

Published by
Purewal Publishing, LLC
176 West Logan Street
Suite #105
Noblesville, Indiana 46060-1437
www.suzannepurewal.com

Cover Art and Design by Joseph S. Anderson – TheForgottenArtist.com
L. E. Hewitt's photo by Marty Moran – whitehotheadshot.com
Suzanne Purewal's photo by Hether Miles – hethermilesphotography.com

ISBN: 978-0-9829048-6-2 (print version)
ISBN: 978-0-9829048-7-9 (e-book version)

Library of Congress Card Catalog Number: 2017951637

Printed in the United States of America

A dedication page recognizes the individual or individuals who have inspired the author in some fashion. However, this book has two authors, with different sources of inspiration. We considered dedicating the book to each other. However, that appeared a bit unseemly.

After some thought, we considered dedicating it to all of the frogs we kissed and all of the fish we threw back in the sea, via our catch and release program.

In that playful spirit, we dedicate this book to those we met along the way on our journeys to find one another. We would not have been able to fully appreciate each other without you.

Additional Titles by L. E. Hewitt

Life Between the Raindrops
My Wonderful Chaos
Chasing the Silver Lining
I Don't Have a Button For That
My Bucket List Has A Hole In It
Free TP and Frog Cures

Additional Titles by Suzanne Purewal

Embracing Destiny
Challenging Destiny
From 14 to 41
Mis-Matched to Miss Matched

Preface

What you are about to read is a, "He Said/She Said," account of the zany, unexpected courtship between two authors, L. E. Hewitt and me, Suzanne Purewal. I can guarantee that you have never read anything like it.

This project was his brainchild. I will admit, I was leery at first. How could we possibly write a book together? Our speaking and writing styles are vastly different. Although, as our work progressed, I realized that is exactly what makes this book so funny and flow so well.

What do I mean?

Picture a woman, from Upstate New York, with twelve years of Catholic school education, with a penchant for rules, who is deathly allergic to all animals, finding her soulmate in a multiple cat-owning, rule-hating guy, who grew up on a farm in an extremely rural mountain town in Pennsylvania.

Basically, we are, *The Odd Couple*, amped up on steroids. At times, his class clown antics frustrate the dreamy, hopeless romantic in me. As a result, our differences lead to lively, interesting, and entertaining conversations. There is never a dull moment.

This book chronicles our budding relationship with our quirky senses of humor and a liberal dose of sarcasm. His chapters are the odd-numbered chapters. Hence, my chapters are the even-numbered chapters.

I wholeheartedly agree that there are two sides to every story. However, I am going to let you in on a little secret—my side is the right side. Eventually, he will figure that out on his own. In the meantime, I will just humor him. It is the path of least resistance anyway. But just don't tell him that!

Chapter 1

I need to name her. She has suddenly appeared in my life, and I honestly believe that she is meant to be here for a long, long time. So, I need to name her. I name everyone that I write about. It is a way to protect their identity and also a way for me to claim ignorance if they ever try to sue me for any hypothetical likenesses in my books.

Now, what shall I name her? She is so sweet and smart and gorgeous and funny and … and … She is just everything I could have ever asked for, from what I can see so far.

Francesca! Hmmm, that one is classy like her. Mary! No, that just doesn't feel right. Claudine! Doesn't sound exciting enough. This name choosing can be hard work. Ah, I have it—Isabella! Classy, beautiful, and Italian, just like her!

Now, you are probably wondering, "Who is Isabella?"

That story began about thirteen months ago. It was November, and the annual Christmas gift event for hobbies and crafts was taking place just down the road a few miles at the state fairgrounds.

This was a very large gathering of vendors selling their wares to people who were getting a head start on their holiday shopping. I didn't particularly need anything, but I enjoyed snooping around. I do recall that I almost bought a hoverboard that day. I tested one. It was lots of fun. However, I then remembered that I am in my fifties, and when I fall down nowadays, it hurts a whole bunch more than it used to!

Among the hundreds of booths I visited that day, one caught my attention. It was a local authors' booth. Of course, being a writer myself, I was drawn to the books, exploring their subject matter.

Seated at one of the tables was Isabella—a dark-haired, blue-eyed, stunningly attractive woman in her mid-forties. We authors are frequently not a very pretty bunch, so this beauty certainly stood out from the usual crowd. I am betting that is why she couldn't keep her eyes off of me either. I am such a handsome buck! She even had a bit of drool on the side of her mouth, and she kept looking at me like I was the last piece of pie at a Weight Watchers convention.

I chatted with her a bit. She even talked me into buying a book. Next, she wanted my contact information. She said she wanted to discuss me joining this event in the future with my books, but I am no dummy. I knew she was up to something! I wasn't sure what, but it was something!

I never forgot Isabella. Her photo graced the back cover of the book I had purchased, and every time I came across that darned book, I would pause to look at that picture and be reminded of just how beautiful she was. This could have been where the story ended, but little did I know what was about to unfold.

Chapter 2

Isabella, huh? Okay, I can live with that name. I have been called worse. His memory of the day's events is a bit muddled, but let's chalk that up to creative license.

It was Friday, the 13th. (Cue the dramatic music.)

I was handing out bookmarks with my poems on them and rattling off my thirty-second spiel to passersby on why their lives would not be complete until they had read my books.

This tall, handsome man appeared intrigued by my books, or it might have been the hint of cleavage in that day's outfit. Nevertheless, he purchased my poetry book and informed me that he, too, was a published author.

Excited by the prospect of getting to know another author and having him participate in the show, I used my extroverted nature and charm to convince him to join us the following year. Or then again, it might have been the cleavage.

I do not recall any drooling on my part. A lady does not drool. And I hate pie. I am more of a chocolate cake, chocolate torte, or a warm, ooey, gooey brownie type of person. Although, I might have licked my lips as my mind said to itself, "Ooo, he's yummy."

Anyway, I think he needs a name too. I narrowed it down to

Lars and Lancelot. Upon careful deliberation, I decided on Lancelot. (Insert a trumpet flourish here.)

And time passed …

Exactly one year later, on Sunday, the 13th, as I set up the booth for the last day of the Annual Christmas Gift & Hobby Show, at the Indiana State Fairgrounds, I switched the seating arrangement for two of the authors. I can not explain why I did it. It could have been karma or divine intervention. Either way, something urged me to do it. That placed Lancelot next to me.

After five days of hawking books and standing on concrete, I was tired. But I did my best to talk to Lancelot in between engaging potential customers. He seemed quiet and reserved. But when he got going on his stories, his eyes lit up, and he became quite animated. He was witty, contemplative, and most of all, he made me laugh. And when Lancelot mentioned he was from Pennsylvania, I knew we would be great friends. Being from New York, us East Coasters always seem to find one another, and we get along splendidly!

We discussed getting together to chat about writing sometime. Authors and poets do that sort of thing. That helps us feel less misunderstood and that we don't belong on the Island of Misfit Toys.

With an hour left in the day, my boyfriend showed up. That put a damper on chatting with Lancelot. Yes, I had a boyfriend. However, we had only been dating for two weeks. So, it was not a serious relationship. And deep down, I knew his days were numbered. He had issues, and we did not have common interests. Anyway …

When the show ended, my fellow authors helped break down the booth and pack everything in my SUV. During this chaotic flurry of activity, Lancelot reminded me about getting together to discuss writing. I told him we would have to schedule something soon, and we all went our separate ways.

Around Thanksgiving, Lancelot contacted me. My parents were in town. So, I told him we would get together after they left.

More time passed …

On December 13th, Lancelot posted a funny meme on his Facebook page. I sent him a message commenting on it. And so, the banter for our fated meeting began.

Chapter 3

First of all, I need to set the record straight about this 13th thing. Isabella was telling me how the 13th is an evil day. "Nothing good ever happens on the 13th!" She said that she was diagnosed with cancer many years ago, on the 13th. She was downsized from a very good job, on the 13th. She was arrested for belly dancing without a proper license, on the 13th.

She simply felt it was a very unlucky day, and important activities should be avoided. That is until I, yes, *me*, showed her the calendar and provided the proof that we actually met, for the first time, on Friday, the 13th.

From there, her investigations discovered that we had again ended up at the same event exactly one year later, on the 13th. Next, exactly one month later, on the 13th, she contacted me, via an instant messaging service, to hatch her plan to snag herself a bachelor!

Now, I had originally planned to meet her at a coffee shop to simply gain some extra knowledge of the local authors' scene. It was a purely professional endeavor. By the time she was through with me, I was meeting her for dinner at a fancy restaurant. She played me like a fine fiddle! I was okay with that, since she was awfully cute and all.

I figured, what the heck? She couldn't be any stranger than some of the other dinner dates I have endured in my life.

So, the plans were finalized, and the appointed evening arrived. If I recall correctly, we had a 6:30 P.M. reservation. She arrived slightly before me and was waiting in the lobby when I entered the restaurant. I must admit that she did indeed look stunning! She was obviously pulling out all of the stops to catch me.

The conversation flowed easily. The poor server had to come back multiple times before we were even looking at the menus. Isabella obviously couldn't take her eyes off of me, and I kept staring at her too.

It was a great dinner. The food was excellent, the server was patient, and my company was absolutely delightful. Five hours later, being the only people left in the place, and with an ice storm raging outside, we stood up and made our way toward the exit.

Little did I know that my life was about to change forever. Little did I know that I was about to be transformed. It is amazing how you can blindly be approaching a major life event and yet be totally unaware that it is coming. Isabella and I both made it to the front, and I summoned the valet. He knew which two cars were ours. They were the only two left in the icy parking lot. We waited just inside the front doors for him to return.

Chapter 4

O kay, I have reevaluated the ever-present number thirteen as it pertains to my life. Instead of viewing it negatively, I will consider it in a positive light. Major life-altering events occur in my world on the thirteenth of any particular month. As one chapter ends, another begins. A death and rebirth. A phoenix rising from the ashes, if you will.

Thus, enters Lancelot, stage right.

For the record, I have never attempted belly dancing. He must have confused that with my pole dancing adventures. But that's another story for another day.

Lancelot is correct concerning the fact that I did not want to meet at a coffee shop. First of all, I do not drink coffee. I drink tea or hot chocolate when I'm sick. And I was not sick. For the most part, I drink water. Room temperature water to be precise.

And did I mention that the weather report was calling for an ice storm that evening?

So, I said, "If I am going to risk life and limb to go out in this weather, it's going to be for dinner."

I expected this to be a business meeting, and we would go Dutch. I suggested Olive Garden. I had a gift card *and* a coupon.

He countered with a corner table at White Castle.

I responded, "Oh, hell no!"

Then he surprised me with his suggestion for an upscale restaurant.

I eagerly agreed. "Good choice. They have valet, so I won't kill myself crossing an icy parking lot. Perfect!"

He inquired, "Does your boyfriend not have an objection with you having dinner with a handsome man like me?"

Rolling my eyes, I replied, "We broke up. So, it's not a problem."

"Wahoo! Er … I mean, sorry to hear that."

Interesting response. Okay, Isabella, play it cool.

He then informed me that he made reservations at 6:15 P.M., under Clooney and McAdams.

Right then, I knew he was going to be a handful. But that was nothing compared to the conversation we had concerning what he would wear to this grand meeting of the minds.

The options he presented were: Hawaiian shirt, bicycle shorts, a kimono, or a kilt.

In that spirit, I recommended a Speedo or perhaps a Harley jacket and chaps. Two can play that game!

In the end, we were both appropriately attired. The meal and company were wonderful, as he stated. Time flew. We could have talked for hours more, but the restaurant closed early due to the dangerous weather and road conditions.

We huddled inside the doors waiting for the valet. I stood facing Lancelot, shivering. My pretty winter coat was not constructed for warmth. It's just pretty. He, on the other hand, had no coat and was perfectly comfortable. The man is a human furnace.

Evidently, that radiating warmth made him completely irresistible. Before I knew it, I leaned toward him, and he leaned toward me. Our lips met, and we kissed.

It was a truly magical kiss.

I thought, *This is my last first kiss.*

As we parted, I gazed into his eyes. We did not speak. Instead, we kissed again.

I believe I uttered, "Oh, wow!" at some point.

Then, the valet snapped us back to reality.

Seriously, kid? You couldn't have warmed up the cars a little longer?

We had not even gone our separate ways yet, and all I could think of was when I would see Lancelot again. I also hoped that the connection was not just one-sided.

So, I prayed a Rosary as I drove home. Half of it was to make sure I made it home alive, and the other half was that Lancelot wanted to see me again.

The icy roads were treacherous. I drove 15 M.P.H. the entire way. Banged up cars littered the highways and ditches. However, I was determined. I had to talk to Lancelot again.

Oh, who am I kidding? I had to kiss those lips again.

Chapter 5

Once again, her memory of certain events is just a tad bit off. Let me provide the appropriate details for you. First of all, belly dancing, pole dancing, I knew it was some sort of dancing that had landed her in the slammer.

Secondly, I was really going to wear my bicycle pants to the restaurant. But every time I go out in public in them, women stare and throw themselves at me and stuff. It's kinda embarrassing. Besides, I really wanted Isabella staring at me and not my pants.

As for making the reservations under Clooney and McAdams, that was for privacy concerns. We certainly didn't need the paparazzi lurking around trying to be the first to get pictures of us together. I really try to avoid making the front page of the *National Enquirer*.

The first kiss? Ah yes, she was after me like a hound dog chasing a rabbit! I could see it in her eyes! I was just standing there being a good Catholic boy, waiting on my car. The next thing I knew, she was latched onto me and had me paralyzed in a lip lock! Now, I am not saying that I didn't thoroughly enjoy it! Matter of fact, I saw stars and fireworks and flying pigs … and unicorns!

Suddenly, I realized that maybe, just maybe, what I had been searching for so many years, was now standing right in front of me with her tongue in my mouth. Dang, she was cute! Dang, I was feeling like the happiest man in the whole state of Indiana! That's when I saw the valet kid standing in the rain beside my car, holding my door open, and waiting for me. Danged kid!

The drive home that evening was indeed treacherous. There were wrecked cars everywhere on the interstate. I just took my time and carefully navigated my way.

Meanwhile, my mind was swirling. What in the world had just happened? What was that ticklish feeling in my spine? Who was this girl, and where had she been hiding? I was floating on air. I was indeed hopeful for the first time in a very long time. I had all but given up on finding anyone who made me tingle. Yet, just when I least expected, there she was.

I kept asking myself, "What's the catch?" There had to be something bad that I was missing. Then, I recalled a prior conversation that the two of us had shared. She was severely allergic to cats, as in throat-closes-up, could-kill-her type of allergic. Yep, she was allergic to cats, and I currently shared my home with five of them! So, I hurried home and put their little asses out on the front stoop and told those furry freeloaders that they needed to go find a new place to live!

Now, now, hold on! I was kidding about kicking out the cats. FuzzButt would have reported me to the SPCA in a heartbeat. And besides, they are a part of my family. Also, I like challenges, and I wasn't going to allow this challenge to stand in the way of me finding out more about Isabella. There is always a solution. It was Friday. I knew that her parents were coming in on Tuesday to stay for a couple of weeks. I understood that this meant I probably wouldn't get to see her again until they were gone. I was now suffering from a pouty lip.

Chapter 6

Lancelot, a good Catholic boy? Seriously? Who is he trying to kid? First of all, he is not Catholic. And friends, if I had to guess, I would assume he was firmly entrenched on Santa's naughty list.

I, on the other hand, am a good Catholic girl. I graduated from a Catholic grammar school and an all-girls Catholic high school. I even sang and played guitar in my church's Folk Group for thirteen years. Huh! There's that number thirteen again. But I digress …

The following morning, my mind fought with itself. It does that sometimes. The hopeless romantic side was thrilled and jubilant at the thought of finally finding a man who shared so many interests, was witty, and seemed perfect for me.

However, the realistic, pragmatic side played like a broken record. "He has cats. Plural. *Five freaking cats.* He's never going to give up those cats. There is no way this is going to work."

Yes, friends, I am deathly allergic to animals. My reaction is anaphylactic, and my throat closes up. Therefore, exposure to just one cat would literally kill me, let alone an entire clowder of them. That would cause instant death! And it would not be pretty.

The debate in my head ensued, "But we're both authors and musicians. We both sing. He loves live theater. He has season tickets to the symphony, the local dinner theater, and other independent venues with a wide variety of musicals and theater productions."

That right there was enough to make this girl swoon.

My optimistic romantic side continued, "We're both from the East Coast. So, we understand each other. We like parks and traveling. We don't drink much alcohol. And we prefer room temperature water. What are the chances of that? Come on, Isabella. Give the guy a chance."

Quite the conundrum.

For the moment, the hopeless romantic prevailed. Hence, I agreed to a second date on Sunday at a local Mexican restaurant.

The food was delicious. The conversation was thought-provoking. We tossed around the idea of seeing a movie. However, he wanted to stop by a home improvement store first.

Okay. But if he purchased duct tape, plastic sheeting, and zip ties, I was ready to run!

Truth be told, walking around after eating Mexican food was a grand idea as far as my gastrointestinal system was concerned. Refried beans have a way of creeping up on you sometimes. Anyway …

What transpired at the store was slightly odd. He paraded me around the store, searching for people he knew. And then one-by-one, he introduced me to them. Everyone was glad to see him and share the latest news and/or gossip.

As the outsider looking in, he was one well-liked and popular guy.

I had the sneaking suspicion that he just wanted to show off his new arm candy to his friends. So, I held his hand, smiled, and batted my eyelashes on cue. I'm good like that.

We decided to forgo the movie and talk instead. And talk we did, for hours and hours, until we were hungry again. Chinese food was on the menu for dinner.

As the evening wound down, we engaged in another kiss.

I swear that there was something in Lancelot's kisses that interrupted all rational and logical thought. *Drugs!* That must be it. He's drugging me somehow! Why else would I be falling for this guy?

Granted, he is handsome and a nice guy. But I would have rejected him if I came across him on an online dating site. He has five death-inducing torture devices. And he was out of my age range.

But the mind-altering drugs worked their subtle magic much too well. Suffice it to say, after that mind-numbing kiss, Lancelot secured another date.

The nagging voice inside my head pestered, "But what about those cats, Isabella? Don't fall for him. You're only going to end up hurt and alone, again. He won't pick you over the cats. You've been through this before. And you know the definition of insanity is doing the same thing over and over and expecting a different result. You're going to regret this. He will never get rid of his cats. They're family. Get out now. Save yourself from a broken heart."

You know something? I really hate that practical, logical side of me. So, the hopeless romantic side quieted it, and the rest of my body's rumblings, with some delectable pieces of Ghirardelli chocolate.

Chapter 7

Yep, Isabella was so smitten after that first date that she couldn't wait to see me again! If you recall, the initial meeting was on Friday. Her parents were arriving on Tuesday. Somehow, she managed to squeeze me in both Sunday and Monday. The girl had it bad for me. But, can you blame her? I am a hottie! Of course, she was easy to look at too. I am not denying the facts! I like to be accurate about things. She is indeed arm candy.

So, Sunday and Monday were both filled with lots of talking and getting to know each other. We were never at a loss for words, and we were discovering just how incredibly similar we were. It was quickly becoming apparent that this was a significant beginning.

I was starting to sense that this was "her." By "her," I mean the girl that I had been searching for all of my adult life. I truly didn't think she existed. I thought she was like a unicorn. Had I found my unicorn? There was still much to learn, but I was cautiously hopeful.

I needed to still check out a few things to see if she was my match. I knew at some point, I would need to check her for hairy warts. Can't have any of those! I also wondered if she could yodel, a very important attribute, important stuff like that.

So, after spending three days out of four together, it was time for the parents to arrive for their two-week stay. I was planning to see Isabella once or twice during that time. They would be busy with holiday and family stuff the rest of the time.

I was invited to meet the parents on Wednesday, five days into our relationship! This girl obviously had it bad for me! Can you blame her? I *am* a hottie!

The parent meeting went very well. They loved me! They had been worried that their daughter would end up with some worthless chump, so seeing me made their hearts swell with joy. It was a Kumbaya evening.

If my memory serves me correctly, I was then invited to spend Thursday, Friday, and Saturday evenings with the fam! We went out to dinner most of those nights. I was being fed steak and taters and was being buttered up as the man to take their daughter off of their hands.

By Saturday night, I was already the favorite child, placing me ahead of Isabella and her brother. I accomplished this with charm, flowers, chocolate, and cake, not just for Isabella, but for the parents too. I was the sweetest Catholic boy they had ever seen!

Chapter 8

Poor confused Lancelot. His timeline is a touch off. I did not see him on Monday. He had a family dinner with his kids that evening. And he made some sort of cheese balls.

Yuck.

Our next date was on Tuesday, right before my parents were due to arrive.

I may have been smitten, but I'm still sticking to my story that his kisses somehow drugged me and rendered me helpless.

He met my parents on the seventh day, which incidentally was a Thursday. They loved him. That's a good thing, for the most part. But now, I'm thinking it's not his kisses. It's some sort of mind-control or hypnosis. My parents are not pushovers nor are they easily fooled. I'm leaning toward a super-secret plot involving mind-control. Time will tell.

We then spent Friday and Saturday together as a foursome. And Saturday happened to be Christmas Eve. So, after dinner, we sang Christmas carols for a couple of hours.

I played guitar. Lancelot was a professional drummer. So, he played the toy drums we had. Mom actually turned them over to him without fuss. She and my aunt always played the drums during

Christmas carols. They used my guitar case as a drum for years before we finally went out and bought toy drums. Instead, Mom and Dad happily shook sleigh bells. And an absolutely wonderful, melodic time was had by all!

We decided to let my parents fend for themselves the day after Christmas. Lancelot took me to one of my favorite restaurants for sushi. We saw a movie afterward.

December 27th is Mom's birthday. Lancelot presented Mom with a beautiful bouquet of flowers and two of his books as birthday gifts. He also graced me with one dozen long-stemmed red roses.

Does this guy know how to win women over or what?

Dad joked, "No flowers for me? Well, I'm feeling left out."

The next day, Lancelot showed up with two pieces of cake, just for Dad.

Dad thanked him. "I'd rather have cake than flowers any day."

That night, we had dinner with close family friends. And the following night, I met his daughter, Elizabeth, and her fiancé, Donald. We had dinner and saw the *Star Wars* movie.

Apparently, I passed the initial meet and greet test. His daughter invited me to the next family game night.

The following evening, Mom and Dad had to fend for themselves yet again. Lancelot took me to the popular dinner theater in town, and we saw a hilarious live show.

I know by now, you're saying, "You're glossing over all of those days with no details. We want details!"

Well, friends, we were chaperoned the majority of the time by my parents, his daughter, or throngs of people. There was a great deal of talking and getting to know one another. It was lighthearted and fun. We just enjoyed our moments together and each other's company.

Meanwhile, back at the ranch …

While we were painting the town as a twosome, my parents were reading his books. So, upon our return, they were able to thoroughly interrogate him about a variety of topics.

That will teach me to leave them home alone.

My parents knew a great deal more about his life at this point than I did. That fueled the beginning of the playful banter between him and my parents.

Joy of all joys!

I'm sure Lancelot will cheerfully expand on that in his rebuttal.

Oh, lucky, lucky me! Not!

However, I will tell you a little about New Year's Eve. As boring old people, we stayed in. Big gatherings of boisterous, drunk people don't interest any of us. We made hors d'oeuvres and tried to figure out who all of the entertainers were on *Dick Clark's Rockin' New Year's Eve*. We could not identify all of them and concluded we were definitely old. Anyway …

At about fifteen minutes before midnight, I made an announcement. "We're going into the living room now."

My parents and Lancelot looked at me quizzically.

I explained, "I don't want to see you people kiss, and I know for sure you don't want to see us kiss."

My mother replied, "You've got that right."

I grabbed Lancelot's hand and dragged him kicking and screaming into the living room. His protests stopped when I threw him on the couch and told him I was going to have my way with him.

His eyes grew wide as he anticipated what would be next.

"Silly boy, I'm just going to kiss you."

I could tell he was disappointed.

But seriously, what did he expect with my parents in the next room?

Midnight came and went. We were still engaged in a passionate kiss when my mother yelled, "We're coming through. We're going to bed now."

I pulled away from Lancelot. He's hard of hearing, so he didn't know why I pulled away. His eyes conveyed confusion.

"My parents are going to bed. Mom announced they're walking through."

"Oh."

I giggled. Then I shouted, "It's okay, Mom. You can walk through."

"Okay. I just wanted to make sure you heard me."

Laughing, I responded, "I heard you. Thank you."

As they moseyed by, they said, "Happy New Year! Love you!"

I replied, "Love you, too! Good night!"

And thus began the year of hope, good fortune, love, and happiness—2017.

Chapter 9

So, chaperoned dates at my age are not exactly what I would have expected. But, there I was face-to-face every evening with the mom and the dad. I guess I should name them too! I like naming people! Let's see, Francesca and Carl. That sounds good.

I have to admit being treated to successive steak dinners was a perk. Meeting some friends of Suzanne's, another perk. Spending Christmas Eve and singing Christmas carols with people I had known for a week, now that was certainly unique.

As I look back, I now believe that Francesca and Carl were in on this from the start. I believe that Isabella had informed them about this super hunky, author guy that she had met, and I think they hatched this plan as a threesome! They saw me for the wholesome bachelor that I was, and they carried out a concerted effort to take advantage of my wholesomeness. That's what they did, I tell ya!

Isabella was correct that she took me into another room and attacked me on New Year's Eve. Her parents just sat there and let it happen! Sure sounds like collusion to me, not that I am complaining or anything.

Francesca and Carl were around for a few more days after the new year. We got to spend much quality time together. They were reading my books and growing to love me more and more! Did I mention what a wholesome Catholic boy I am?

On what was probably our final evening out to dinner, Carl proclaimed that he would be in favor of me taking his daughter's hand. I was pondering this thought for a bit. I was deciding which hand would be most useful to me. Yes, I am kinda slow sometimes, but then it hit me! They were trying to marry me off already! I'm telling you, it was a conspiracy! They were working together to play me like a fiddle!

Now, don't get me wrong, Isabella is cute and all, and she has many redeeming qualities. Although, I can not list them all here since her parents might read this book, and I do not wish to jeopardize my favored child status. But, let me just say that she was certainly a good catch. But marriage? That's a commitment of at least a couple of years! Also, it's expensive to get out of those! But, she certainly was cute and a great kisser!

Anyhow, FINALLY, er ... I mean, finally, the day came for Francesca and Carl to return to Florida. I was certainly gonna miss them. We had such fun together.

Ah, but now Isabella and I were about to be unchaperoned for the first time since day three of our relationship! Let the wild parties begin! I was scared! This lonely, desperate woman was now left alone with all of my hotness. I'm not sure if I told you already, but I'm a hottie! I wasn't sure if I could keep her at bay enough to maintain my favored, wholesome, Catholic boy status. The struggle was real! Now, I'm not saying that I was complaining or anything. I was just concerned for my pristine reputation.

Now, don't tell Isabella or Francesca or Carl this. You have to promise. I am going to peel away the layers and tell you what was going on inside of me at this point. Somehow, some way, as completely irrational and crazy as it sounds, I had managed to fall head over heels in love with a woman in two weeks. There was suddenly no doubt. I knew where my future was headed. My heart felt at home.

This woman was so like me that it was difficult to grasp. We were both writers and musicians, had similar political and social views, we shared a quirky sense of humor, and yodeling. All of these great qualities, perfect for me, wrapped up inside a physically stunning woman, and she wasn't trying to get away or filing for one of those pesky restraining orders or nothing!

I could not have custom-ordered anyone better, well except for the cat allergy thing. I would have changed that. Oh, and the wash your hands every time you come in the house thing. Well, actually, I can humor her with that one.

Of course, I don't have any weird quirks. But if I did, I'm sure she would accept them too. Now, remember, not a single word about this, because nobody is supposed to fall madly in love in two weeks!

Now, where was I?

The first weekend alone with Isabella, after her parents had left, I spent a lot of time crying and feeling sad because I missed Francesca and Carl.

See? I know how to maintain my favored status by putting stuff like that in a book.

Actually, we spent a considerable amount of time kissing on the couch like two convicts who had just escaped from prison. We were now beginning to discuss where we were going to go from here. There was much to discuss.

Chapter 10

Good news! Mom granted her seal of approval on her new name. She says it sounds beautiful. However, Dad's alter ego has been, "Zeke," for years. Ergo, from henceforth, he shall be referred to as, "Zeke."

What Lancelot didn't know was that we were part of a clandestine government spy agency experimenting with a full-immersion technique to ensnare, oops, find me a husband. The family experience, including chaperones and family holidays, were crucial elements of this mission. We had to evaluate his survival skills.

An item of note: Lancelot's persistent claims of being "Catholic," "good," and "wholesome" continue to be worrisome. Further investigation into these delusions of grandeur is warranted.

A second item of note: Francesca and Zeke did not technically grant Lancelot the coveted "favorite child" status. Lancelot crowned himself with that title, and they did not correct him.

At this point, I must admit, I was struggling. I wanted to dare to dream about a future with Lancelot. But my practical side had constructed a wall, due to the cat menagerie situation.

My annoying logical side would not let up. "How could you let yourself fall in love with a man with five cats?"

The romantic in me replied, "Because aside from the cats, he is perfect for you. Never, ever have you met a man like him. You have hoped, wished, and dreamt about finding a life partner like him. You even bargained with God to send you a man who shares your interests, eagerly encourages and supports you in all that you do, and even provides the occasional kick in the rear."

Dear readers, I indeed searched high and low for, "The One," for years and was utterly unsuccessful. I had given up all hope of ever finding him. I cancelled all of my online dating accounts. I seriously considered moving to a different state. I was convinced I would never find anyone here in the Midwest. I thought I would go work in a National Park somewhere with mountains, trees, and pristine blue-green lakes.

Then God messed with my head and threw Lancelot my way.

Thanks, God! Thank you for sending me the equivalent of a wonderfully decadent chocolate cake, only to be able to look at it, but never enjoy a single morsel.

For some reason, God loves to torment me. Either that, or somebody put the evil eye on me. Those are the only logical explanations for this cruel and heartbreaking scenario.

Lancelot sensed the wall and my reservations. He reassured me that the cats would not be a problem. He would find a workable solution, come hell or high water.

That, Isabella, is why you have fallen for Lancelot. He is, "The One." He claims he will move heaven and earth in order for the two of you to be together. And you believe him. Your heart is telling you that you can trust him. His word is his bond. He means what he says.

I hear one of my close friends saying, "Told you so! Didn't I tell you that you would find someone once you stopped looking?"

But let's be real. My head convinced itself to stop looking.

However, it's obvious, my heart and soul did not. And I will be forever grateful that was the case.

Now to address his quirk comment. For the record, washing your hands after you enter the house is not a quirk. Doesn't he remember anything from his childhood? I'll bet Lancelot's mother told him to wash his hands and the rest of his dirt-covered or mud-caked body all the time. He's just having a convenient mental block at the moment.

And let's not forget television mothers. Every quintessential television mother ordered their children to get cleaned up and/or washed up, especially if they were about to eat dinner. I have generations of mothers and television history on my side on that one.

Now, if I started hosing Lancelot down in the driveway before allowing him to enter the house, that might be quirky. Or it might be kinky. Sometimes I get those words mixed up!

Chapter 11

So, she says she gets quirky and kinky mixed up! Well, okay, then do I have some quirks to share with you! Except, I can't. Francesca will probably read this book, and remember, I can not jeopardize my favored status. Besides, this family treats those subjects with a "don't ask, don't tell" policy. We do not discuss those details. I guess that's the Catholic way. You just wait, and go tell the priest, and he forgives you. I have also learned that it is smart to go to the old priest that has early dementia, because he will forget your sins before he leaves the confessional.

On the quirk front, I do need to share Isabella's gas pumping rules. You fill the car up even after the auto shutoff cries uncle. Then the total cost must end in a zero or a five. Curious, I asked why. Her response, "Because, I just like it that way!"

After pumping the gas, I got into the car and attempted to scratch my nose. Isabella burst into action, pulled my hand away from my face, and handed me an antibacterial wipe. I played along and wiped my hands. I then thought I would really impress her and wipe my face too. She just shook her head. I am not certain, but I am guessing I wasn't supposed to do that either.

See? I got sidetracked again. So, Isabella and I had started discussing our future plans. It was seeming more and more likely that we were going to stick together for the foreseeable future.

We decided to work out a schedule. I was to leave her house by 9:00 P.M. on weeknights, so that by 10:00 P.M., she could be in bed. She likes to rise early and be productive before the chickens.

I, on the other hand, prefer to let the chickens get their eggs laid before I contemplate rolling out of bed at the crack of 9:00 or 10:00 A.M., and then I get better as the day goes along, with my most productive time coming between midnight and 3:00 A.M.. So, technically, I am up earlier in the morning than she is.

This whole plan didn't work out so well at first, because Isabella kept begging me to stay when my time to leave came. However, me, being the adult, I was a good boy and made her stick to her schedule. I'm sweet like that.

When it came to naming her parents, I knew that I would face rejection. I was prepared for this. I was informed that, "Carl," would actually become, "Zeke." I guess it was a false name he had used in a Canadian prison during a family vacation gone awry. I wasn't given too many details. Personally, I am calling him, "Z-Dawg," because we are tight like that.

Now, back to this quirkiness. Isabella keeps an immaculate house. No shoes. Wash your hands. My daughter, Elizabeth, and her fiancé, Donald, joined us one night for a game night, and Donald commented that the house was the cleanest he had ever seen. I was a little bit hurt by this considering that he has seen my bachelor pad many times. The cats and I keep things purrfect. Well, not really, but don't tell Isabella. Remember, she can not come to my house for fear of death, so all she needs to know is what I tell her.

I know that she was appalled by my answer to a game question regarding how many times a month I wash my sheets. I don't think

I need to scare her by telling her how often I make messes, or forget to put stuff away, or that I don't own any antibacterial wipes. That's our little secret, okay?

I am learning so much about Isabella as we roll along through life. She has elfin toes. She is apparently allergic to my shaving cream. The hair on her warts grows at an alarming rate. She doesn't like cheesy breath. All sorts of important stuff to know! But, she is so smart and so kind and so giving and so talented. She enhances my life in immeasurable ways.

Chapter 12

In my defense of hand washing and/or the use of antibacterial wipes and gels, it is cold and flu season. Healthcare professionals stress the importance of washing your hands often and that you should avoid touching your face. So, after touching a gas pump that a zillion people have cootied, you should clean off your hands.

Since when is it a quirk to have a clean house? Everyone I knew growing up had a clean house. No one wore shoes indoors. I take that back. There were two houses in which I didn't remove my shoes. God only knows what was growing in those shag carpets. One house was so filthy, I would never eat any food they served. I feared for my life and longed for a hazmat suit.

In many cultures, it is customary to remove one's shoes upon entering a house. There is a long list of them, including Canada, Denmark, Greece, India, Russia, South and East Asian countries, Middle Eastern countries, and yes, the United States, particularly Hawaii and Alaska. So, it's not something that I dreamed up as a conspiracy against the footwear industry.

A friend once declared that if he had to have surgery, he'd have it in my house because it was so clean. What's funny is that I'm the messy one in the family. Mom and my brother were always neater than me.

We're not counting Dad. Messes seem to follow him everywhere. Poor Dad.

I know Lancelot is messy. Off-the-charts, run-for-the-hills, epic tsunami messy. There is plenty of pictorial evidence to support it. Not to mention the amount of Shout stain remover I'm using on my poor tablecloth. Or the time I spend cleaning the floor around his chair. I'm considering covering his eating area and the floor with plastic. It would make clean-up so much easier.

And I do not want to rehash the whole bedsheet washing conversation. It gave me the heebie-jeebies. I'm having nightmares about it. I might be scarred for life!

Something else that might have scarred me for life was his cheesy burps. He had eaten almost his weight in cheese one night. The cheesy breath that resulted was bad enough. But the burps? Certifiable weapons-grade gaseous third circle of hell kind of torture. Yuck and double yuck.

Speaking of torture, while my parents were still here, Lancelot asked them for a list of my good qualities.

Dad rattled off loyal, dependable, intelligent, loving, etc.

Thank you, Dad.

Mom temporarily lost her mind and said, "She has funny toes."

Loudly, I exclaimed, "Ma!"

She laughed. "What? I was trying to be funny."

"You don't have to be funny! He's going to write about it. You're killing me."

Intrigued, Lancelot implored, "I must hear more about these funny toes."

Heavy sigh.

Mom was laughing her head off.

Dad looked at her bewildered. He was still trying to marry me off and couldn't believe Mom was sabotaging all of our hard work.

No more wine for Mom. I cut her off.

I answered, "Fine. I have flat feet, and my big toes turn up slightly."

Okay, so the not-so-secret secret is out. I have odd-looking feet. Big whoop-dee-doo!

Let's get back to quirks. Believe it or not, Lancelot has some of his own quirks.

These quirky things could also fall into the category of: "You know you need to spend more time with people and less with animals when …"

In the beginning of this budding relationship, every time a song came on that he loved, he would heed the urge to play drums.

The problem was that he used my body as the drum set. My head was the cymbals. I felt as if I was in a martial arts battle. I threw up my arms to block the onslaught of blows. And I protested vehemently. "My body is not to be used as a percussive instrument!"

Sure, it's all fun and games until I lose an eye or end up with a concussion from repetitive head trauma.

One of his persistent quirks is how he treats me like one of his beloved animals. Almost daily, I have found myself being patted like a dog. But that's not bad compared to the scratching.

Lancelot will lovingly put his arm around me. Then while cuddling, without warning, he will start scratching my arm like you would scratch a cat or dog.

I don't have fleas, so I don't need to be scratched! My skin is delicate. His manly fingernails are mangling my clothes and marring my porcelain skin.

Repeatedly, I remind him, "Use the pads of your fingers, not your nails!"

If that doesn't sink into his brain soon, I just might turn into a fierce animal. I am woman, hear me roar!

Well, I would love to tell you more. However, I need to go spot clean the rug before whatever he just dropped becomes a permanent stain.

All I can say is that he's really lucky that he can yodel and kiss well.

Chapter 13

My, my! She is just rambling on about this and that. I don't know where she dreams up her version of events. Yes, I do scratch her. Those hairy warts look itchy. I can not just leave them alone. I need to scratch the tops off, so the puss can escape.

So, how often do you wash the bed sheets at your house? Well, I did a little Internet research. One in twenty of us Americans wash the sheets once every four weeks. Most of us do that chore every two to three weeks. Isabella and her mother do them once a week. And some weird old retired microbiologist, who is retired in Maine, does hers daily.

I have a good pattern for these things. I always know that it's sheet washing day on the day I change my underwear. Now, on the opposite weeks, I wash the pillowcases and take a bath.

I did find one site that said to wash your sheets at least once a week. However, I want to share with you some other bits of wisdom that were listed there as well. I can not make this stuff up, folks! This is amazing stuff.

For instance, you should NEVER wash your jeans. Yep, you heard that right, never. It allows the color of the denim to become bespoke to those who wear them. Now, you know I didn't make that up, because I don't even know what "bespoke" means! The website is: www.goodtoknow.co.uk. Look for the Wellbeing Section. Search for: How Often Should You Be Cleaning and Ditching Everyday Items?

Here is a tidbit for you to chew on. You should replace hand towels every two uses. Who the hell does that? Isabella leaves hers up for a month in the downstairs bathroom. She is *killing* me!

Here's another, toss out the Tupperware every three months. My mother had some pieces that were probably older than me, and I am still alive.

Emery boards. Three uses, and they should hit the trash.

Dish cloth. One week, then in the trash.

Cutting boards. Twelve months, and then throw them away. Apparently, a cutting board can contain 200% more fecal bacteria than a toilet seat. Yum!

Wooden spoons. Five years. My mother's never lasted that long. They were worn out much earlier from beating me with them.

Razors. Five uses. That's it. I'm not sure how I am supposed to afford this one. Maybe five months would be more reasonable.

House slippers. Clean as often as possible. Throw away every six months. I have a pair in my closet that is at least twenty years old.

Kitchen sponge. Clean every day, and replace once a week. I thought you just waited until stuff was visibly growing on it.

New clothes. Wash them before you wear them. But, then they are not new, and what about those new jeans I am never supposed to wash?

However, it is okay to wear a bra three times between cleanings. What? That doesn't make sense. Aren't boobs all sweaty in the summer?

Washing machine. We are supposed to clean the washing machine twice a month with a toothbrush, hot water, and vinegar. It says that for a spruce up in between, you can drop a dishwasher tablet in there, and let it rip. I can throw that in when I wash Isabella's clothes. I am environmentally-friendly like that, saving water ya know.

I am not certain what a tea towel is, but I am supposed to clean it daily.

Pajamas? Two days, then into the wash.

They also recommend cleaning the toilet once a week. I actually hose down the inside of my toilet bowl several times a day. Oh, that's not how you are supposed to clean it?

Wash your purse or wallet once a week. Uh, I have never done this, ever.

Clean your pillows every three months. It would seem to me that I get way more gunk on my pillow than my sheets.

Steam clean your mattress every six months. Uh, again, let's not discuss this one.

So, now my question becomes, if I do all of this stuff, when am I gonna have time to do anything else? I mean, I won't have time to mow the yard, or take out the garbage, or go to work, or change the oil in the car, or …

You know, maybe it is indeed time for a lifestyle change! I sure hope Isabella knows to use 10W30.

Chapter 14

One thing is for certain. Lancelot will never, ever be allowed to wash my clothes or be in charge of laundry. He would shrink and/or ruin all of my clothes. I would end up with nothing to wear.

Oh, wait a minute, that's probably why he wants to do my laundry. Well, forget it, Buster, I'm on to your sinful plan to have me run around naked all the time. Good Catholic boy, my ass!

That is definite grounds for him losing his favorite child status with my mother. She is against all nakedness. When I was in the hospital, she walked behind me holding the back of my gown together. God forbid the nurses saw my underwear. But I digress …

Seriously though, he should be overjoyed that I will do all of the laundry. That's one less thing for him to do. Actually, it should be counted as more than one task considering the heaping mound of filthy clothes he generates in a day. It's so bad at times, it's enough to make the Baby Jesus weep!

And after reviewing that list of his, I will be in charge of all of those things. So, he will have tons of free time to do all of the tasks that need a man's touch.

Translation: He will be doing tasks that involve dirt, grass, weeds, shrubbery, and snow removal. While we're at it, let's throw in power washing and staining the deck for good measure.

I am sure, given enough time, I can develop quite a list to keep Lancelot busy and out of trouble. He is going to need it, especially since he won't be able to blame the mysterious mishaps on the cats anymore. Just imagine a whole new world with no more lost socks!

As far as the 10W30 is concerned, for my vehicles, it had better be 5W30 and synthetic. Lancelot should know better than to mess with a woman who worked in the automotive industry for twenty-two years. I know how to do a lot of automotive-related things. I just prefer to pay someone else to do them. But if Lancelot doesn't want to pay to have the oil changed in the vehicles, he can assume that duty as well. It's his choice.

Okay, there's something that's been bugging me since we started this literary odyssey. And I can't stay silent about it any longer. It's driving me crazy. Why do we have fake names?

My name is on the front cover, and my picture is on the back cover. It's not as if we're writing porn. In that case, I would definitely have to write under a fake name. Otherwise, my mother would have a conniption fit, then a stroke, and perhaps a massive coronary on top of it.

I can hear her now, "Oh, my God! I am completely disgusted and mortified! What possessed you to do such a horrible thing? Oh, my God! What will everyone say?"

My answer would be, "I'm guessing no one you knew would say anything, because they would have to admit to buying and reading smut in the first place!"

I understand the need for him to create names for other people he writes about to avoid getting sued when they read about themselves and don't like it. But this is different. We are writing this together.

So, Lancelot, why are we referring to ourselves in this book under fake names?

Chapter 15

Okay, folks, you heard it right here. She said she is gonna follow ALL of these guidelines for cleaning and throwing out stuff. I can only assume this includes the no-wash-jeans rule and the scrub-Lancelot's-back-twice-a-week rule.

As for the fake names, I only named Isabella that so when her mother reads the book, she will not be offended. Normally, I would call her my sexy love muffin. I didn't think Mother would approve. However, I guess I can go with her given birth name, Leroy … oh, um, I think she is saving that surprise for a future "tell all" book. So, most people call her, "Suzanne." So I will go with that for the moment.

I am learning more and more about Love muf … er, I mean, Suzanne, all the time. Just the other night, we went to a musical called, *Once*. It was filled with exceptionally talented musicians, singers, actors, and dancers. I was thoroughly enjoying the show, until halfway through the second act. The male lead was performing a love ballad when Suzanne suddenly leaped up and rushed the stage. Security had to forcefully remove her as she threw various undergarments at the beleaguered performer.

Tickets to the show had cost me $84, and I spent an additional

$525 in bail money to get her released. I had no choice since her mother left me in charge of keeping her precious daughter out of trouble. I would not wish to jeopardize my most favored status.

Suzanne also likes to tell me how to drive. She says she is in fear of being maimed when I am behind the wheel. I keep telling her that I have not maimed a single soul yet. If I look at her for a split second, she points angrily at the road ahead. If I take my hand off the wheel to scratch myself, she admonishes me. If I play my turn on, "Words with Friends," while passing a semi-truck on a narrow two-lane road, she gives me a dirty look. She says I cross the center line too often. I tell her I am just avoiding potholes. She is also always informing me of the current speed limit in an area. I am of the belief that as long as I can outrun the local police, speed limits are merely suggestions.

But, you know, with all of these "issues," Suzanne is still the best thing to have come along in my life. She is smart and funny and kind and giving. She lets me know how wonderful I am, and I humbly agree with her. We are off to a great start. I know that I still need to get her properly trained in many areas, but this will be a labor of love. I will have her whipped into shape in no time at all!

Chapter 16

Yes, dear readers, I am strongly compelled to instruct Lynn on highway and city driving. Someone else failed miserably teaching him that critical skill set back in his teens. His biggest challenge is maintaining his lane. Dotted and solid lines have no meaning and are invisible to him. I don't dare take my eyes off the road for a moment. His eyes are everywhere except the road.

I swear to God I'm going to throw his cell phone out the window. One afternoon, we were driving downhill on a curve. His eyes were glued to his phone. Neither of his hands were on the steering wheel. We crossed the center line into oncoming traffic. If I had not grabbed the wheel, we would have hit the oncoming car head-on. After a mini-lecture from me, he claimed he was steering with his knee, and we would have been fine.

I think not! I saw the impending doom, took action, and averted the crisis. *That* is why we are fine. *Sheesh!*

At times, I know he is just trying to relive his glory days of being the five-time, All-County Off-Road Driving Champion in the state of Tennessee. Those were lawless days when he learned his rough and tumble maneuvering techniques while running moonshine in the hills. That is, until he blew up the family still, burned down four acres of mature trees, compromised his competitor's moonshine operation on the edge of said trees, went on the lam, and escaped to "Honest To Goodness" Indiana.

Truth be told, he was way more afraid of the wrath of his neighbor, Jim Bob, over compromising his lucrative moonshine operation, than getting captured by the police.

That completely explains why I feel as if I am in an episode of *The Dukes of Hazzard*. But Lynn won't slide across the hood like Bo and Luke Duke. He's selfish that way.

And the worst part of it all is that Lynn refuses to wear tight jeans and cowboy boots like the Duke boys. He complains tight jeans don't have enough room for all of his stuff.

He does have a point there. The first time he took his stuff out, my jaw almost hit the floor. I was simply amazed.

His pants' pockets produced a wallet, a myriad of receipts, loose change, a cell phone, a ring of keys any maintenance man would be proud of, a Swiss Army knife, a treasure map, a set of Allen wrenches, a paint brush, a phone charger, a roll of duct tape, the manuscript for his next book, a chew toy, two AA batteries, and a lint-covered granola bar.

Oops, how did I get so far off track? Well, let me rein it back in. I was commenting on his exciting career in moonshining and running from the law before the whole tight jeans thing took over.

Those rough and rowdy Tennessee days also made him impatient. That impatience has gotten out of hand. Just the other day, he swerved up onto the sidewalk to bypass slow traffic in town. An elderly lady threw her cane at Lynn's car to demonstrate her displeasure. Her husband shouted obscenities and shook his fist. Children saw him coming and ran for their lives. Poor children!

I have considered purchasing a racing helmet. And I've asked him to install suicide handles. (Those are grab bars mounted inside the car.) But does he listen? No!

So, do I instruct and/or lecture Lynn on safe driving, keeping his eyes on the road, and having at least one hand on the wheel? You bet I do.

You see, I come from a long line of lingerers. And I have years of suffering and lingering left. I'm going to outlive everyone. I just know it! That's why I am afraid of being maimed in a car accident.

And you would think that Lynn would want to avoid maiming me at all costs. He thinks I'm nagging him now? He should imagine hearing, "I told you so!" every day, multiple times a day, for the rest of his life.

Despite his crazy quirks and bad driving, I still love him. Lynn is a great guy and has lots of fantastic qualities. For example, right now, he is making me dinner. How awesome is that?

I'm going to check in on him and see how things are going. I'm so lucky to have such a thoughtful, caring, loving, and …

"Oh, my God! There's water everywhere! And there's tomato sauce on the floor. Geez, don't step in it! You'll track it everywhere."

Oblivious to the mess, he asked, "What? Where?"

Heavy sigh.

Sorry, friends, I have to end this now. I have an entire kitchen to clean. Every surface is covered with water, raw sausage drippings, and pieces of onion. The special rye bread we went to a bakery to buy is sitting in a puddle of water. I hope there's not a hole in that bag. Otherwise, he will be eating soggy rye bread.

But it's okay. I still love him. He is perfect for me and a truly wonderful guy. At least that's what I keep telling myself.

Chapter 17

That woman must be drinking again! A few tiny droplets of water on her kitchen counter and a meal fit for a king served to her, and yet she thinks the kitchen exploded! And what's with this whole moonshine story? I didn't run moonshine when I lived in Tennessee. I was an exotic dancer, and she knows it! She just seems to be playing loose with the facts, unlike me.

I remain a fine, upstanding, good Catholic boy. You can trust me. I am always helping little old ladies cross the street and watering my neighbor's lawn, and I even stand on the corner handing out money to strangers.

Suzanne, on the other hand, writes romance novels, and they have sex scenes in them. I don't know where she learned all of that stuff, and I don't think I want to know either. Meanwhile, my books are all about children and puppies and happy things. That's because I am a good boy.

The other day we met my daughter, Elizabeth, and her fiancé, Donald, for dinner at a fifties-style diner. It's a nice place to go for a burger. Suzanne had a burger, French fries, onion rings, and fried pickles! There was food everywhere! We then decided to go bowling. The first place seemed to be problematic for the kids, for whatever reason. We then went next door to an arcade. This was going fine until Suzanne knocked over some five-year-old and stole the stuffed animal he had just won! We were then asked to leave.

Next stop was yet another bowling alley. As we were walking in, Elizabeth tiptoed up behind us and attempted to scare us. Suzanne peed her pants. Luckily, she was wearing her super absorbent undergarment made for women of a certain age.

Once inside, while Suzanne changed her undergarment, I checked on a lane. There was a three-hour wait! Who the heck waits three hours to bowl? That was just crazy! So, instead, we all went back to Suzanne's house and played Skip Bo. We are party animals like that. It was a fun evening.

I know that I have already spoiled this woman for all other men. I am such a catch. She reminisces about her online dating woes sometimes. Men who lied about their height, weight, age, used old pictures from when they still had hair, stuff like that.

So, she had given up with the online stuff when she found me. I have hair. I am tall and devilishly handsome. I have a chiseled body and a radiant smile. I am humble. What more could a girl want?

It's funny. Every time I go to see her, she opens the door with a mischievous grin on her face, kinda like the look I have when the waitress at IHOP brings me a big stack of pancakes and bacon. It feels good to be that loved. It's a good place to be in life.

Chapter 18

There he goes again. Lynn has difficulty keeping track of his tall tales and how they might contradict one another. He claims he was an exotic dancer. But that doesn't mesh well with the whole good, Catholic boy persona he keeps trying to sell you.

He's avoiding the moonshine thing like the plague. There's still an outstanding warrant for him in Tennessee. I don't want to see him go to jail. Neither do his cats. Who would feed them while he was in the pokey?

Although while doing hard time, he would amass tons of new writing material. Imagine the stories that would result from being surrounded by convicted felons, morning, noon, and night! He might even write some blues or country songs. He could become the next Johnny Cash!

Don't let him fool you with his holier-than-thou attitude. News flash! Children are the result of people having sex. And puppies are the result of dogs having sex. Ergo, Lynn can only write his books because of all the sex that's going on.

Yes, I write romance novels. But the sex scenes are tastefully written. They're not "X" rated, nor are they like those poorly written and overrated, *50 Shades*, books. I'm not into violence or bondage.

Although, at times, it seems as if Lynn is itching to get smacked upside the head.

Lynn won't be happy that I'm saying this, but that diner was just okay. The good part about that meal was the company. Sorry to say that the food offerings paled in comparison to the diners back home in New York.

The burger was fine. I ate several French fries, a few onion rings, and one lousy fried pickle. Yes, I said it. One *lousy* fried pickle. One was enough. Pickles are meant to be eaten in their natural state, from a glass Vlasic pickle jar.

The adventure after dinner made me believe we were participating in a treasure hunt, devised by Donald and Elizabeth, without a map, clues, or compass. Lynn and I followed them blindly, plotting to steal the treasure from them at the last minute.

Alas, there was no monetary treasure to claim. However, the true treasure turned out to be a great evening with the kids. And I will take that any day of the week.

Lynn's right. He is quite a catch. His list of attributes is impressive. He has a full head of curly hair that he attempts to straighten. For the record, I prefer it wild and wavy. It gives him a sexy vibe. He's an accomplished musician and published author. He is a human furnace and never needs a coat. He leaves a mess wherever he goes. So, if he gets lost, I can easily find him. That particular feature will come in handy as we grow older.

But it's the way he slouches that turns me on immensely. I mean really, who wants a guy who stands up perfectly straight, head held high, with his stomach sucked in and his chest pushed out? Slouching is all the rage this year. And Lynn has that look down pat. Now we can add "trendsetter" to his list!

So, back off all you brazen, single women! This hot, handsome, lovable guy is all mine!

Chapter 19

First of all, if she thinks the best pickles come from a Vlasic pickle jar, then she has some real issues. But, I will be able to retrain her on that, so I am not worried. That is a minor issue. However, when it comes to storytelling, this woman takes the cake.

Did you know that she claims that she has never lost a sock? Never! Never, ever, never! Now, I don't know anybody who could proclaim such a thing with a straight face. I personally own a whole drawer filled with orphans. I believe that the rest of the country is right there with me. Speaking of which, I just had a grand idea. I should start an orphaned sock website! People can post pictures of all of the lonely little fellers, and perhaps we can find some of them new mates!

I need to work on that. It's gonna be a viral smash! I will become an Internet billionaire and buy me a motorcycle with a sidecar for Suzanne!

Anyhow, I will get started on that right after I finish telling you what's been on my mind. It's this whole name thing. First, she called me, "Lancelot." Next, she changed it to, "Lynn." There are actually a few other names I have gone by in the past as well.

My ex-wife often called me, "Jesus Christ." This was usually followed by, "Are you that stupid?" or "What were you thinking?" or something to that effect.

My mother called me, "Dammit." I often heard, "Dammit, come here!" or "Dammit, where are you?" or "Dammit, get your ass in the house!"

I have been called a few other things that a good Catholic boy like myself could never repeat as well. But, those people all seemed to have anger issues.

Suzanne does call me, "honey," often, and she has even called me, "God," a time or two, but I am not allowed to talk about that either.

A few people do call me, "L. E.," since that is the name I put on the cover of my books.

In my books, as I have mentioned, I do change people's names. What I find interesting is how many people actually embrace their new names. Some will call me on the phone and identify themselves by their assigned names. This is usually followed by some swearing and threats of legal action, but yet they still seem to enjoy the names.

I do take the time to try and pick appropriate names for most of my subjects. There were a few where I had to settle on alternative choices. My publisher seemed to frown upon names like, "Lying sack of shit," and "Bitch with a bad hair weave." So, I had to play nice a few times.

As for Isabella, I think that is a good second name for Suzanne. It rolls off the tongue nicely. It just sounds better than, "Neatfreak," or "Germophobic Sophia." Isabella is a beautiful name, and Suzanne is a beautiful woman. So, even with all of her quirks, she deserves a fitting name.

I am going to agree with her on one topic. I am indeed the absent-minded professor. I get involved in the things I am doing, and then something else pops up in my head, and I go do that. Next, a third and fourth thing will appear. Suddenly, I have forgotten about the first thing and have lost all of my tools along the journey. I spend lots of time looking for stuff.

And yes, I will never be able to successfully wander off as an old man. My trail of odds and ends will follow me. And yes, I do keep many things in my pockets. That's what they are for.

Let's see, currently, I have a wallet, keys, a phone, a small Phillips screwdriver, an electrical tester, a receipt, two AA batteries, some lint, three dollars, a nickel, a quarter, a small piece of wood, so that I can match the thickness at the store, and an allergy pill. I do not see this as an overabundance of stuff! Plus, it's all important stuff!

Suzanne thinks I need to have a little basket. Um, I think that's called a purse, and my racquetball buddies would make fun of me!

Chapter 20

I think the orphaned sock website is a great idea! Although, I would have no need to visit that site. I have never lost a sock. I don't understand how they get lost.

If all of your socks were accounted for prior to putting them into the washing machine, and then you transferred all of the washing machine's contents to the dryer, when the dryer was done, all of your socks would still be there.

I guess there could be a sock puppet master lurking outside, in desperate need of colorful characters that would make perfect sock puppets. This demented puppet master would wait for the right moment. Then bam! He would steal socks for his upcoming performance.

More likely, it's pets. From what I understand, pets steal anything and everything they can get their little paws on. So, if a human accidently drops a sock before, during, or after the washing and/or drying process, it will join the black hole of try-to-get-it-and-I'll-scratch-your-eyes-out socks.

Children in sports or who live in multiple residences would be more prone to losing socks. The lone sock could be on a playing field, in a locker room, on the floor of a school bus, in the trunk of a car, at the other parent's house, or at the best friend's house. You see where I'm going with this.

I honestly think that's how the current non-matching sock trend started out. Kids gave up on finding matching socks, so they just grabbed whatever was available. And *Voila!* A new trend was born. Good job of making it work, kids!

For whatever reason, Lynn just can not let this name thing go. What's in a name? Shakespeare answered that question in, *Romeo and Juliet*. And we all know how tragically that ended. So, when choosing names, choose carefully!

My name is Suzanne. That's what I prefer to be called. I mean, it *is* my name. Bella means beautiful in Italian. So, I can live with that too. Unless you're thinking about that girl in the *Twilight* movies. If that's the case, forget it. Stick with Suzanne. It's better that way.

Over the years, people have called me a wide variety of things. Let's see what I can remember. The ones I didn't mind were: Q, Sue, Angel, Princess, Suzanny, Suzanna Danna, Moneypenny, Snow White, Pollyanna, Poozlet, Mami Ji, and Bhabi. (Mami Ji and Bhabi are Punjabi for Aunt and cousin's wife, respectively.)

Then there were other ones: teacher's pet, nerd, geek, stuck-up, brown-nose, goody-two-shoes, bitch, surf board, and poodle ears.

All I have to say about the second list is, "Sticks and stones may break my bones, but names will never hurt me." Oh, I now have larger breasts, so "surf board" doesn't apply anymore.

What the absent-minded professor needs is a freaking tool belt. It would have places for his tools. He wouldn't lose/misplace them anymore. What a time-saver! In addition, it would save his pants' pockets from being overloaded and dragging down his pants to reveal the ever-dreaded butt crack. It's not a pretty sight. And bonus for me, Lynn can start wearing tighter jeans!

The basket idea was for a hypothetical situation. If/when we get married, he can't keep all of his stuff on the bathroom vanity. I told him I would get him a toiletries basket to put under the sink. He won't misplace or lose anything, if it's all together in one place.

You see, I am a problem solver. I am determined to solve all of Lynn's challenges. Or die trying.

Chapter 21

I really don't see why she feels she needs to give me a cute little basket in the bathroom. I may as well just turn in my man card. I can just spread my crap out on my side of the vanity, and everything will be just fine. It's all about functionality, all of my tools at my fingertips, not in my man basket.

It reminds me of a guy I did audio/video work for many years ago. His wife had a wicker basket for his remote controls in his man cave. I just went ahead and neutered him and got it over with. He no longer deserved to be a man.

Now, back to this bathroom thing. Suzanne's master bath has a double vanity. She is adamant that she MUST have the left side. She is right-handed, I am left.

Wouldn't it make more sense for me to take the left one? But, no! She insists and says that I am just being silly. So, I reminded her that great relationships are built on compromise. I asked her, "What do I get if I give up the left sink?" She told me that I get the basement and the third bay in the garage as my domains.

Now, wait a minute! That just doesn't sound like a fair tradeoff! She wants to ban me from the kitchen, restrict me to the right sink in the bathroom, and forbid me from ever doing laundry. This list of rules just keeps getting longer! I will get her back! When she is gone to the store, I will go upstairs and shave in her sink!

But wait, I nearly forgot something. When we were at the grocery store, Suzanne asked me what kind of cereal I would like to have. I replied that I was fine, I could just eat her Total. She then said that she thought I liked Cheerios. I told her that I do, but I also like Total. She then replied, "But, my Total costs almost twice as much as the Cheerios!" Apparently, I am not worthy of the expensive cereal!

The whole grocery store trip was a bit unusual. First, we drove around one parking lot. Suzanne explained that since there were no open spots in the first three rows that we were not supposed to shop at this particular location today. The next store was apparently more acceptable. But first, let me back up.

Before the regular grocery store, we went to one of those discount warehouse stores that sells all kinds of stuff. As we walked past a stack of queen-sized mattresses that were on sale, Suzanne asked me if I wanted to get banned from the store today! Of course, a good Catholic boy like me was shocked to realize what she meant by this! Now, where was I? I keep getting sidetracked.

Okay, so back to regular grocery store number two, the one I actually got to go inside. We compared her favorite peanut butter versus mine. Mine was definitely better, but we bought both. She got the wrong brand of orange juice without even consulting me, and she even kept hopping on the back of the buggy and riding it like a kick scooter down the aisles. This woman is gonna take a lot of training!

I do have to say that we did have a nice time after we returned back to her house from the store. She put the groceries away. I helped by unbagging everything. I'm sweet like that. We then sat on the sofa and talked, and she made fish lips at me. It was a nice night.

Chapter 22

If Lynn doesn't want a cute little basket, that's fine. I will buy him the ugliest medium-sized basket I can find. And crap belongs in the toilet, and only in the toilet. If he spreads any crap on my vanity, God better help him!

For the record, Mr. I'm-Throwing-a-Tantrum-Because-I-Want-the-Left-Sink would smash his elbow against the wall and medicine cabinet if he attempted to brush his teeth over the left sink. There is not enough room for a left-handed person to use the left sink.

The right sink is perfect for him because it provides plenty of room for him to brush his teeth, trim his wild and wooly nose and ear hairs, and tame that uncontrollable mane of thick wavy hair.

I can not believe that he is complaining about being relegated to the basement. Poor pitiful him getting 1,245 square feet of space that's all his. Some people's houses are smaller than that. Come to think of it, there is an entire television show devoted to those crazy tiny house people!

To me, that show is like a clown car in a circus act. Let's see if we can fit two people, their bicycles, two large dogs, and all the stuff from a 1,200-square-foot house into 500 square feet! Madness, I tell you!

And I'm also giving him part of the garage. For whatever reason, that's still not enough. He is a greedy man. Always wanting more.

He is welcome to shave in my sink as a revenge tactic. But in reality, he will be only hurting himself. He'll be icing his bruised elbow. And his face will be dotted with scraps of toilet paper from all the cuts sustained from hitting the wall while shaving.

For the most part, I have always done grocery shopping by myself. It is a much quicker and peaceful process that way. Shopping with Lynn is like shopping with an inquisitive, hyper two-year-old. I swear I only took my eyes off of him for a minute while comparing the ingredients of products, and he wandered off. I had to spend the next five minutes searching for him.

When I found him, he said, "Oh, I thought you knew I would be over here."

Right, because I developed some sort of ESP in the last few minutes.

I think I'm going to have to install that app on our phones that parents use to track their kids. That way, I'll be able to find him. It's either that or a harness. Then I could literally keep him on a short leash.

I know I don't have to worry about anyone kidnapping him though. After dealing with him for about an hour, they would bring him right back.

Yes, my Total cereal costs twice as much as those bland Cheerios. He never said he *liked* my cereal. He said he could eat it. Being able to tolerate a type of food is a far cry from liking it. And he proclaimed his undying love for Cheerios in a previous book. This goes to show you that I read his books and paid attention.

I suggested he buy the cereal that he loves because I want him to be happy. Instead, he threw another one of his tantrums in the cereal aisle. A three-year-old boy approached him with a box of Froot

Loops in one hand and a box of Pops Tarts in the other, in an attempt to comfort him. Lynn rejected the boy's kindness, growled at him, and then grabbed a box of Kashi cereal.

For the record, Lynn's peanut butter is not better than mine. His brand has molasses in it. I do not want molasses in my peanut butter. I want peanuts in my peanut butter.

The other bad things that he mentioned were things he did. He's the one who jumped on a mattress in the middle of the store and suggested I try it out with him. Sorry, I like that store, and I don't want to be banned from it for life.

And he was the one who took a running start with the shopping cart and jumped on it. The front of the cart wasn't heavy enough, and it popped up. He pleaded with me to jump on the other end to provide a counter-balance. I think he just wanted me there as a cushion for when he hit the stacked packs of water bottles.

The rest of the evening was very nice, and informative too. Among other things, I learned he can roll his tongue. But he needs to practice his fish lips technique. It's not very good.

Tomorrow I'm going to see if he can do the Vulcan hand gesture for, "Live long and prosper." Then maybe we will play a game of Rock Paper Scissors Lizard Spock.

Chapter 23

Boy, I don't know where she gets some of her ideas. I try to convey to you, based in fact, how this relationship is going. Yet, she just goes off on these wild tangents playing loose with the truth. It's a good thing you have me around to keep the record straight. I would never steer you wrong.

We are planning a Super Bowl party this coming Sunday. I watch the game. Suzanne watches the commercials. Elizabeth and Donald are coming over too. When we were deciding on a menu, I sought their input. They wanted pizza rolls and dinosaur nuggets.

Suzanne looked at me as if I had lost my mind. She typically would make various appetizers containing shrimp and crab. But Elizabeth is allergic. Elizabeth would typically make items containing cheese. Suzanne is lactose intolerant. I offered to install a TV for her in the bathroom. Suzanne wasn't so crazy about that idea. Personally, I thought it was brilliant. I could even install one of those bass shakers on the toilet, so that it would vibrate with the crowd noise. I'm handy like that.

Since this relationship has lasted more than a week or two, and we kind of seem to like making fish lips at each other, we have started to discuss some possibilities about how this life might work long-term.

I own five cats. Suzanne will die a horrible death if she stays in a room with a cat. She can not live in a house that has previously ever had pets. She can not share a heating and cooling system with them. Everything must be separate. My cats are mostly elderly and are indoor cats.

I offered to build Suzanne a shed out in the backyard. She just gave me "the look." Guys, you know the look I am talking about. We've all seen it at one time or another. I was reading where those "she sheds" are all the rage. I thought it would be a nice place to keep her.

Another option is to find a pet-free house with a mother-in-law apartment. I felt this idea had merit until I realized that Suzanne wasn't planning on living in the mother-in-law's quarters. I mean, there's me and five cats, and then there's just her. I know you can see my logic.

The other option under consideration is for me to buy a second house, a small house, in the same general vicinity as her house. It would become my own personal cathouse. Suzanne even says that I can stay there some nights. She probably means the nights when she finds my behavior unacceptable, or she is simply tired of looking at me. I have the feeling that she may send me to the cathouse frequently.

Of course, all of these plans are hypothetical. Hypothetically, I may someday ask her a certain question, and hypothetically, she might be suffering from some sort of temporary insanity and say, "Yes," to said question. You just never can tell about such things.

Chapter 24

I have given up trying to debate facts with a man who embraces truthiness as much as Lynn does. To deal with his alternative version of the facts, I often follow the advice of nurses caring for dementia patients—just play along, so you don't upset them.

I bet Super Bowl Sunday is the single most unhealthy food day of the year. However, I was still surprised by the kids' request for pizza rolls and dino nuggets.

I asked, "What are dino nuggets?"

"Chicken nuggets shaped like dinosaurs."

"Seriously?"

"Yes."

"They can't eat regular shaped ones?"

"Donald likes the dinosaur ones."

"Okey dokey then."

I have never seen nor eaten dino nuggets. I've only eaten McNuggets. And I haven't eaten a pizza roll in over twenty years. But if that's what they want, that's what they'll get.

While at the store, Lynn also grabbed Doritos, a nut mix claiming to be a hunter's mix, whatever that means, salami, two types of olives, guacamole, tortilla chips, salsa, two jars of cheese dip for the chips, a cheesecake sampler with several flavors of cheesecake, and two hunks of cheese. Are you sensing the cheese theme with this family? And he rounded out the shopping cart with crackers and franks in a blanket.

I'm confused though. What happened to the pigs? Did they fly away? Or did the franks kick them out of their warm cozy blankets in a hostile takeover?

Just food for thought!

My arteries hardened just viewing the contents of the cart. To placate my poor arteries, I opted for veggies and a healthy snack mix of chickpeas, fava beans, and pumpkin seeds.

While driving home, I tossed around the idea of ordering Indian food for game day, so I would have something to eat. You should have seen the look Lynn gave me on that suggestion.

It's not as if I would make him eat it. In fact, I would eat it all myself! However, the Indian restaurant is too far away and doesn't deliver.

The hypothetical living situation is a serious topic. My allergic reaction to all animals is anaphylactic. Suffocating is horrible. Not to mention the angst associated with being injected with enough rounds of epinephrine, Benadryl, and steroids to knock over a horse. And you could cut the tension with a knife watching the ER staff hover over me hoping I won't die. I have been saved numerous times by the hard-working ER staff at my local hospital. Thank God for them!

And I have said enough Rosaries to stretch to the moon and back. Then throw in the Rosaries and Novenas said by my parents, family members, and friends. That's at least another two trips to the moon and back.

Imagine all of those heroic measures to save me, plus the prayers and special intentions for me, and God decides to answer by sending me a guy with five cats. So, either God hates me, or He has a warped, twisted sense of humor.

Nevertheless, there will be a house for the cats. Where it will be, and how this will work, I have no idea. But Lynn says he will figure it out. Time will tell!

Of course, this is all hypothetical. I have not been asked *the* question yet.

However, that might happen sooner than I had originally thought. Tonight, he took me to the Indian restaurant for dinner. Afterward, we went to several jewelry stores to look at engagement rings.

The salesperson at the store where we spent the most time said I should become a diamond grader. I can spot flaws and inclusions with my naked eyes that other people need magnification to find. You see, I would rather have a smaller, perfect diamond than a larger flawed one.

And now I know if this author thing doesn't work out, I can go into the diamond business. They are a girl's best friend after all!

Chapter 25

Apparently, Suzanne has not attended many Super Bowl parties in her life. Dino nuggets and pizza rolls sound like normal fare for such an event to me. Of course, I am a lifelong Steelers fan, so we have lots of practice at celebrating championships.

Now, don't get me wrong, Suzanne understands the game of football just fine. She just doesn't understand the entertainment value of some 300-pound defensive lineman driving the full force of his body on top of Tom Brady so hard that he has to go to the sidelines and change his pants.

Now, see, when it comes to her commentary about the Indian food, once again, I need to correct the record. Ms. Purewal, did I indeed take you to the Indian restaurant on Saturday night? Miss Purewal, did I object to going to said restaurant? Ms. Purewal, did I appear to enjoy my meal including the chutney sampler, the mashed taters and peas baked inside of a thing that resembles a mini-Stromboli shell, and the little donut thingies in syrup?

She doesn't seem to realize that I indeed love to eat various cuisines. I may not know the proper names of the dishes, however, my waistline says that I like food! I am likely to eat just about anything that doesn't eat me first.

When I was young, my metabolism permitted such behaviors. I was super skinny. Nowadays, even water makes me gain weight. I'm just lucky that Suzanne likes fat boys like me.

Now, this whole jewelry store thing was to just keep her guessing. It also was an important information gathering mission for me. I might get around to hypothetically asking her some sort of question sometime over the course of the next decade. So, as a seasoned bachelor, I wanted to see how much this hypothetical question might cost me. She queried me about a budget. I said, "Fifty bucks." Apparently, her definition of the word, "bucks," differs slightly from mine.

The jewelry woman would pull out a stone and place it on this black velvet thingy. Suzanne would pick up the lighted magnifying glass, take one look, and say, "Better," meaning, she wanted a better diamond.

Who knew there was all of this stuff about cut and color and clarity? I am left to conclude that Suzanne has spent many years in preparation for this moment. She was more of an expert than the sales lady!

She claims that she is not a "jewelry person." Well, she was spouting out words like occlusion, carbon, cleavage, GIA, and AGS. This old country boy was way out of his league!

In the end, since the Hope Diamond wasn't available, she had made her selection of the highest quality rock that she could find in the store. The size was not huge, but the price had a few more zeroes in it than my bank account.

The sales lady then asked Suzanne to take a walk while she "talked" to me privately.

"You poor man!" she began. "You are gonna have your hands full with this one! Perhaps, I can assist you in finding a woman with poorer eyesight."

I considered her offer for a brief moment, but then I decided that, no, I really like this one in just about every other way. So, I think I will keep her. But, now I know. Now I know that someday, I am gonna need to win the lottery to afford this ring. In my mind, I have already won the lottery by having Suzanne in my life. She is the only prize I need.

Chapter 26

For the first time in history, the Super Bowl went into overtime. Even with that extra time added, I still have enough food left over to feed a small army. My refrigerator is groaning under the added weight. And that's after I pawned off the must-have dino nuggets, pizza rolls, franks in a blanket, and the two jars of cheese dip to the kids. I sent Lynn home with vegetables. No calorically-laden snacks or dip for him.

I enjoyed everyone's wardrobe selections for the game. Elizabeth donned a Steelers jersey. Donald wore a Colts hooded sweatshirt. Lynn sported a bright red Rio Olympic games T-shirt and a pair of shorts adorned with little sharks. Talk about a bold and risky fashion choice.

What about me? I do not own any football or sports-related attire. But I definitely did not want to be mistaken for a Patriots fan, so I couldn't wear red, white, or blue. I opted for a black V-neck sweater. I know, boring. Next time, I'll wear a gold necklace with the black sweater. Then I can say I'm wearing black and gold for the Steelers.

Speaking of jewelry, I never asked to go ring shopping. It would be tacky and uncouth to do so. It was his idea. And no, I was not holding a gun to his head or twisting his arm at the time.

Quality is infinitely more important to me than quantity. That applies across the board, but it is especially true if we are referring to chocolate or diamonds.

I specifically asked the sales lady to see diamonds that were round solitaires, essentially perfect in color and clarity, between one half of a carat and three quarters of a carat. My fingers are long and slender. Anything larger would look ridiculous and fake on my hand. Bigger is not always better.

I am not, and never will be, a jewelry person. During my school and working years, I wore a watch every day. My watch battery died four years ago. I didn't bother replacing it. My cell phone tells me the time.

I added my high school ring starting my junior year and wore it until I married my ex-husband. The wedding rings remained until my ex's midlife crisis, nineteen years later. I haven't worn any rings since.

I will occasionally wear a necklace if I'm dressed up and going out or if I'm doing a book signing.

The only bracelets I wear are plastic and have my name, birthdate, doctor's name, and whether I am an inpatient or outpatient.

I never got my ears pierced. That right there should prove that I am not a jewelry person.

Most often, I find jewelry to be superfluous. When engaged in a conversation with people, I look at their faces, not their jewelry, unless it's bling that's so blinding that I am compelled to locate a pair of sunglasses.

Ostentatious bling does not impress me at all. I am more interested in a person for what is inside his/her heart, mind, and soul.

Hence, when I wear a piece of jewelry, it is a big deal. It is important. And the two most important pieces of jewelry, in my opinion, are an engagement ring and a wedding band. They represent shared promises, hopes, dreams, vows, love, and fidelity.

So the fact that he took me ring shopping speaks volumes about how he feels about me. And the fact that I agreed speaks volumes about how I feel about him. This hot, sexy, handsome, loving, and albeit, messy man truly loves me.

It just makes sense that a perfect ring will represent our perfect union. Correction: our hypothetical perfect union. Well, as in opposites-attract perfect. I will be the neat yin to his messy yang.

However, I have faith that *the* question will be popped in a unique, only-Lynn-could-think-this-up, fashion. I did warn him against putting the ring in anything I would be eating or drinking. With my luck, I wouldn't see it, and I'd swallow it. Then the proposal would be on hold until the ring took a leisurely vacation through my entire gastrointestinal system.

Honestly, I'm not sure I have enough antibacterial wipes or gel for that clean-up job. Let's just hope he heeds my advice and we never, ever have to find out!

Chapter 27

Suzanne is correct when she says that I should never hide a ring inside of a food item that she is about to eat. Have you ever watched *Wild Kingdom* and seen a lion take down a gazelle? Well, that's how Suzanne approaches her dinner. It can be a bit unnerving at times.

Take tonight for instance, I went over to her house for dinner. She had made pork chops and mashed taters. I sat down and began to quietly eat my salad. She came along, plopped her plate down and tore right into the pork chop with both hands! I have never really heard a woman growl like that before. I just kept my head down and kept eating my salad fearfully. I didn't dare make any sudden moves.

Dinner was followed by cheesecake for dessert. You see, I am a smart man. At the store the other day, I looked longingly at this round cheesecake thing with a bunch of different flavors. Suzanne noticed me staring and suggested that we get it for the Super Bowl party. I tepidly agreed on the outside. On the inside, I was saying, "SCORE!"

You see, I knew that Elizabeth was making brownies to bring to the party. So, the cheesecake could remain hidden away in the fridge. Now, it's just me and the cheesecake for the next week and a half!

It would be remiss of me not to mention the sadness of this particular day as well. This morning, as I held her in my arms, my eldest cat of nearly nineteen years passed away. These pets have been a large part of my family for a long time. Angel was her name. She was a great human companion. Of course, Suzanne had never met her due to her extreme allergies. But, Suzanne was there to comfort me this evening in my time of great sorrow. I am a bit sad that the two of them never met. They would have probably been great friends too. I do, however, admire how Suzanne is empathetic to my connection to animals. She has never gotten to have that experience, yet she respects how important they are to my life. This is another reason why I believe that she is incredibly special. She gets me.

Chapter 28

Wild Kingdom, huh? If I had to pick an animal to represent me, I would pick a panther, not a lion. Panthers are sleeker and prettier. And I will bet they are neater too.

I am not the one who eats with my hands and leaves carnage in a five-foot radius around my chair after a meal. Nor am I the one who can pick enough shards of tortilla chips off my clothes later to qualify as a light snack.

I will admit that I eat quickly. Okay, very quickly. I believe it's the result of eating the majority of my meals alone in front of a television for the past umpteen years. It could also be attributed to the fact that I don't like cold mashed potatoes.

Hot foods cool off rapidly if you eat slowly. And before you know it, you are eating cold mashed potatoes and cold everything else.

Restaurants figured this out. That's why servers will warn you not to touch the plate because it's scalding hot.

Come to think of it, I remember my mother pouring boiling water into my thermos to prep it before filling it with soup. It sat in my lunchbox for four hours, and the soup was still warm at lunchtime. Was she smart or what?

My dilemma is that my dishes are not oven-safe. In addition, microwaving an empty plate is not a good idea. Perhaps I will start experimenting with boiling water before buying all new dishes.

Here's another tidbit: I eat to live. I don't live to eat. For the most part, eating is a task that I must complete before I can move on to whatever is next on the agenda.

I hear gasping and other sounds of dismay escaping your lips. Maybe a jaw or two dropped. Others of you will send me your favorite recipes, convinced you will change my mind.

Don't get me wrong, I can savor a delectably decadent chocolate masterpiece. But I will still consume it more quickly than I should. I am a creature of habit.

Of course, this might just be a ploy on my part to get yummy recipes from our adoring fans. You never know!

The loss of a loved one is never easy. Although I have never had a pet, I still understand the profound loss associated with losing a loved one. Loss is loss. And I believe for some people, losing a pet is worse. People walk out on you. Pets don't. They are there, through thick and thin. As long as you feed them, pet them, and give them a nice place to poop, they're happy.

For Lynn's sake and Angel's sake, I am thankful that Angel was healthy and did not have to suffer through a prolonged illness. She lived a long life and made Lynn's life fuller by being a member of his family. That's all anyone needs to understand.

And as much as I respect Lynn's love of animals, I do not understand his unreasonable relationship with bugs.

During dinner, an ugly stink bug repeatedly dive-bombed us. Before I could employ my highly effective smack and smear method, he captured the flying menace in his bare hands. He then escorted it to the front door where he released it back into the wild.

What type of insanity is that?

You know that bug is going to find its way back into my house. And when it does, I will be ready. Lynn is only here a few hours a day. What he doesn't know won't hurt him.

Bugs are outside creatures, and they should remain there. Once they cross my threshold, they are fair game.

The only bugs I don't harm are ladybugs. I like them. Aren't they supposed to bring good luck? I wouldn't dare screw up my good luck chances!

Spiders, bees, and wasps all fall under the category of nemesis. When I first moved into this house, it was infested with spiders. Not the Daddy Long Legs, hang-around-in-the-corner type of spiders, but the large, hairy, black, jumping, running, crunch-when-you-step-on-them variety. We didn't have those in New York. Obviously, Indiana spent years breeding some crazy militarized arachnids.

These monsters would wait on the basement stairs. As soon as I opened the door, they would race up the stairs and come straight at me. Terrified they would slip under the door when it was closed, I stuffed paper towels in the gap, just in case.

When I called Orkin, I explained my plight. I am positive the guy on the other end of the phone thought I was a hysterical woman making a mountain out of a mole hill. They sent a female technician to deal with me.

I brought her to the basement door and warned her to be ready. She laughed and said she'd seen everything there was to see in her line of work.

That was true, until I opened that basement door. The army of spiders charged her. She stomped, jumped, and screamed.

I'm not so crazy now, am I, Orkin lady?

Slamming the door, she exclaimed, "Oh, my God! You weren't kidding. I have never seen spiders do that in all my years on the job."

"Welcome to my world."

She steeled herself and opened the door again. I wished her luck as I closed the door behind her.

You didn't think I was going to follow her, did you?

Thirty minutes later, she emerged sweaty and out of breath. I was glad because I would not have gone down there in an attempt to save her. I would have called 9-1-1. But I wouldn't have delved into that cellar for anything.

And before you judge me, that would have been the scene in the horror movie when you would have been yelling at the girl to not go down those cellar steps.

Oh, in case you were wondering, my smack and smear method is just as it sounds. I use a flip-flop to smack the bug. Then I smear it for good measure. I had to add the smear element after I thought I had killed a bee, only to learn that I had just stunned it. Smearing eliminates any doubt.

That's my motto: Better to be safe than sorry!

Chapter 29

This basement is the very same one that Suzanne is GRACIOUSLY permitting me to have as my very own if we should ever decide to cohabitate. She is probably hoping that the killer spiders will return. I really wouldn't mind sharing the space. I feel that they have as much right to be here as I do.

The ones she described were probably an organized spider army sent to seek retribution for all of the gruesome insect killings that she has performed.

Yes, it is true that I do respect all life in all of its forms. I look at life as a God-given miracle. Therefore, I will do all that I can to preserve it, unlike some people.

I just hope that she doesn't take a dislike toward me someday. I don't want to be smashed and smeared. It sounds horrifically painful.

My love of all creatures comes from my mother. Many times she would bring the car to an immediate halt and order me out of the car to retrieve a turtle. "Dammit, hurry up before a car comes!" she would exclaim. Didn't matter if it was a box turtle or a snapping turtle, it was our job to save it.

I do recall one particular incident on a rural highway. We came around a sharp bend, and there was a turtle right there near the middle, taking his good old time.

Mom pulled off into a nearby driveway and gave me my orders. Just as I exited the car, a big old eighteen-wheeler came around that bend, and it was bye-bye turtle! Mom blamed me for that, saying that I should have been quicker. There was no mention of the fact that I might have been the one smooshed by that big truck. It was all about that poor turtle.

Another reason that I am very respectful of all life is because, having been raised a country boy, I had many animal friends. I had buddies who were cows and sheep and horses and chickens and dogs and pigs and cats and turtles and possums and raccoons and a whole bunch more. I learned that they all have unique personalities and can learn to interact with and trust humans.

Also, as a kid, I held lots of bugs and worms and such. I would study them and their actions carefully. Ants amazed me. They could carry things way bigger than themselves. They worked together when need be, they were huge communities, like a family.

I found that most living things could learn to live in harmony with just a little effort. And yes, I know that some people would think that I am weird for what I believe about life, but it's just who I am. I can not be anyone but me.

Well, I guess that's not completely accurate. I can pretend to be someone else. I can play a part, if need be. Why, just the other day Suzanne was telling me that one of these days I need to dress up in a Batman costume and … OUCH! OH! OUCH! NOOOO! OUCH!

Um, I'm sorry, Suzanne just "informed" me that I am not permitted to share that particular story in public. So, on to other topics.

We are approaching Valentine's Day. It's less than a week away. We are actually going to a dinner theater that evening. We both enjoy live plays, much better than the dead ones. I have already been given some Valentine's gift instructions. No stuffed animals, no blingy jewelry, only high quality chocolate, no Reese's Pieces, or M&M's. That sort of limits my options on my budget.

I guess I could get her a gift card to the grocery store, that certainly says love. Maybe I could fill up her car with gas, more love. She seems to be liking my olive bar olives, the ones stuffed with garlic. I could get her a big tub of those. I should still have some cheesecake left over at that time, I could take out a piece and put a bow on it. So much to think about! She is very special to me, so I need to get this right.

Chapter 30

If we decided to role-play for whatever reason, I wouldn't pick something as common and mundane as Batman. A guy running around in tights and a cape just doesn't do it for me. Give me a clean-cut, handsome man in a tuxedo any day. Or a massage guy with magical hands. Or a serenading troubadour. Or a guy who can make my house immaculate and does windows. Yes! That's it! That is my ultimate fantasy right there!

Goodness! Is it getting hot in here? Or is it just me?

Speaking of turning up the heat, my local grocery store is doing its part. I went shopping this morning. As I wheeled the cart past the Valentine's Day merchandise, I saw the usual boxes of candy, stuffed animals, and other over-priced trinkets.

What stopped me in my tracks was one of the end caps—a colorful and prominent assortment of lubrication products. This display was in the main part of the store, not the personal products area. It stood a few feet from the rows of boxed valentines that kids give to one another.

There was a pleasure gel. Its claim to fame was its ability to cause warming, cooling, or tingling. Another bundled two-pack product said that "his" excites with heat. "Hers" provides a tingling sensation.

Put them together and make sparks ignite, or something to that effect.

Right. Because everybody needs to experience the sensation of a fire-breathing dragon between their legs.

And I am positive that this is not what a guy means when he brags about his girlfriend with the smoking hot body!

I prefer to have my *soul* set on fire. I can do without the fancy pyrotechnics, thanks.

The cooling claim confused me. Nobody wants their jets cooled down before things even get started. Talk about a mood killer.

And any tingling sensations should be generated *au naturale*, without the use of chemicals that could cause all sorts of uncomfortable mayhem.

To me, warming means burning. Cooling means pain. Tingling means itching. The last things I want in or around my nether regions are burning, pain, and/or itching.

And you know there are some idiots who won't wipe off their hands properly before touching their eyes. Their evening will conclude with a trip to the ER. They'll have fun explaining to the hospital staff why their eyes are on fire.

"What happened to you?"

"I got warming, tingling sex gel in my eyes."

I *guarantee* that would be the most memorable Valentine's Day for everyone involved!

I consider the dinner theater tickets to be my present for Valentine's Day. A card would be nice too. Other than that, spending an enjoyable evening with Lynn is a perfect way to celebrate our love for each other. In fact, that is true every day of the year, not just Valentine's Day.

If you are wondering, I do have Lynn's gift. I just have to wrap it. And no, it was not a package of those crazy, burning, itching gels!

Chapter 31

So, yesterday was Valentine's Day. I got to spend my evening with Suzanne at our favorite dinner theater watching, *Joseph and the Technicolor Dream Coat.* The show was fabulous and the company even better. I am such a lucky guy.

Prior to going to the show, I arrived at her house bearing roses and a card. Suzanne had already warned me, "No chocolate, and no stuffed animals!" She also had a card for me. It contained a letter from her about what I mean to her. I was very touched and will treasure that letter always. She also had wrapped some chocolates for me and some kind of burning gel that apparently causes some sort of explosions. I am really not sure what that is for yet. She may need to show me what I am … OUCH! OUCH! OH, GOD NO! OUCH! OUCH!

Um, I guess I wasn't supposed to talk about that either. Every time I try to give you details about certain things, I am painfully reminded that Suzanne's mother may read this book, and therefore, details are forbidden. Apparently, we do not speak of such things!

Now, where was I? Oh yes, the exploding stuff. But, I am not going back there for now. I will private message you the details later.

The one odd thing about this Valentine's Day is that Suzanne did not kiss me, not even once! She has been afflicted with some sort of ailment that has made her lips sore and swollen. The doctor has instructed her to avoid using them for the next month, at least that's the story I am being told. It doesn't seem to affect her eating or talking, but somehow, kissing is out of the question. She has warned me, however, that once this medical situation is resolved, I need to watch out, because she is gonna make up for … Uh, I am getting that look again. I am in fear for my safety, so I will say no more!

I will say that I do feel like the luckiest guy around. I have found such a beautiful, caring, loving, funny, intelligent, giving woman who is as crazy about me as I am about her. I hope that never changes. This has been a life-changing relationship for me, and there are many big things just ahead. I will be able to tell you more about those changes the next time we meet here. But, until then, I need to go. I have some arrangements to make. Shhh!

Chapter 32

I will venture to say that yesterday was the best Valentine's Day I have ever had. I received exactly what I wanted—red roses, a card, and an evening with the man I love. It doesn't get any better than that, especially since I didn't have to cook! And I didn't have to hear anybody express their opinions about how Valentine's Day is a made-up holiday created by the greeting card industry.

The musical we thoroughly enjoyed was entitled, *Joseph and the Amazing Technicolor Dreamcoat.* I wanted to make sure you had the correct name, just in case you wanted to look it up. As you are aware, Lynn tends to play loosey-goosey with details and facts.

Valentine's Day provided the perfect opportunity to tell Lynn what he means to me. As I have mentioned, I am a hopeless romantic. I thank God every day for sending him to me. So, the letter I wrote was a mushy, heartfelt romantic tribute to him. And he better treasure it always. It took me two days to write!

He has brought a fullness to my life that was previously unimaginable. He supports and encourages me in all that I do. He challenges me on a daily basis. And he will also give me the proverbial kick in the rear end when I need it. Everything he does is motivated by love. What an absolute gift he is to me. What more could I possibly ask for?

Well, I could ask for someone who doesn't blab my health issues. After I read what he wrote, I thought, *Everyone reading this is going to think I have some kind of venereal disease. Geez. Thanks a lot, Lynn!*

Let me set the record straight—I do not have a venereal disease!

Lynn was the one who caused this problem in the first place. Despite me telling him he had to be allergen-free, he would repeatedly use products that contained things I was allergic to. Throw in some lingering cat dander and hair from the four death varmints, and that created the perfect storm. So, I had an unbelievably severe allergic reaction on top of an already aggravated skin condition. My face, lips, and neck swelled up and burned like hellfire. I imagine it was like sucking on a tube of that burning sex gel!

God, grant me the serenity to not kill Lynn.

With my lips temporarily out of commission, we shared Eskimo kisses and air kisses. Hey, they're kisses, so they count. And he has some kind of nerve to complain, since this was his fault anyway! There is no pleasing him.

Speaking of pleasing, he better be taking his vitamins and eating his Wheaties. Because if he slides an engagement ring on this girl's finger, he is going to need all of the strength he can muster! I plan to ravish him until … Whoops! Sorry about that. Those lines belong in my next romance novel. I don't know how they ended up here.

Where was I? Oh, yes. When he does get around to proposing, I anticipate that I will accept in an extremely ladylike, "G" rated fashion.

In the meantime, I eagerly await what lies ahead. The love and happiness I have found with Lynn are rare gifts indeed. And if this has all been a dream, I beg of you, please don't wake me up.

Epilogue

Lynn and I debated how long we should make this book. We have enough material for several books. However, I needed to concentrate on getting my solo project released. After that book launched, I returned to this project. Coming up with an ending for our ongoing dialogue was challenging. But I think you will agree that what you are about to read is the perfect ending for this particular chapter in our lives.

The day was June 10th. After a quiet, simple dinner at my house, Lynn asked me to slow dance with him. Since I *love* to dance and rarely get a chance to do so, I eagerly accepted.

He queued up, *At Last*, by Etta James.

I smiled as we embraced. *Did I mention that I love to slow dance?*

He said it was *our* song. I will agree that it is definitely on the short list to be our song.

I enjoyed the dance tremendously and kissed him for the sweet and tender impromptu moment.

Then, before I knew what was happening, Lynn was down on one knee. He produced the ring box and popped it open.

The most beautiful diamond ring I had ever seen sparkled at me. I was stunned. Granted, I had selected the loose diamond from an assortment of loose gems many months earlier. However, I had no idea that he went back and purchased it. But there it was, in all its shimmering glory, in a delicate Tiffany setting. It was breathtaking.

He barely got the words out of his mouth before I exclaimed, "Yes! Yes! Yes!"

After I kissed him again and stopped jumping up and down, I helped him stand back up. It was the least I could do!

Once he was standing, I asked him to put that exquisite engagement ring on my finger.

He happily obliged.

That was a magical moment—a moment where the air was saturated with love, happiness, joy, and hope for the future. And I never wanted it, or those feelings, to end. Suffice it to say, there was more kissing after that.

Some people have elaborate engagement stories. But neither of us are the grand gesture type. He knew that was the perfect way to ask me to marry him. Sweet, simple, and romantic. Just the two of us.

See? Underneath the silliness and goofiness, I knew he could be romantic if he tried. And that makes me happier than I have ever been.

Of course, now I have to start planning my, oops, *our* wedding. I need a budget. And I need to say, "Yes," to a dress! Then I have to figure out when and where. We live in Indiana. But the majority of our family and friends live elsewhere. So many decisions! Maybe we will just elope. One thing I know for sure, the ceremony will be heartfelt and romantic.

Both of us have dealt with more than our share of trials and tribulations over the years. And I am sure life will throw some challenges our way. However, being true partners in life, with unconditional love and support to get us up, over, or through any obstacle, makes all the difference.

If there is one takeaway we want you to have from our odd, yet wonderful story is to never give up on finding love and happiness. We are living proof that dreams really do come true.

About the Authors

Author L. E. Hewitt is a product of the rural Appalachian hills of southwestern Pennsylvania, where he was raised in a family filled with love, laughter, hayfields, music, tater gardens, cows, cats, pigs, dogs, horses, and possums. What more could a feller ask for?

As an adult, L. E.'s musical dreams took him to Tennessee where he was able to fulfill many dreams as a studio and road musician before finally settling down to raise a family and run a business.

By his mid-forties, he was chasing a new dream. Now, seven books later, he is still bringing laughter and a positive outlook to his readers.

Suzanne Purewal grew up in Webster, New York. She began telling stories at a very early age and perfected her writing skills and sarcastic wit in high school and college. She worked in the automotive industry for over two decades before her creative side decided that enough was enough.

Since leaving Corporate America, she has published several books. Her most recent release chronicles her hilarious misadventures in online dating. Her series of romantic suspense novels contain a mixture of mystery, romance, and humor that create exciting adventures for the characters and readers alike. Her poetry book contains a soulful blend of love, loss, whimsical, and inspirational pieces.

Finally! An Unexpected Love Story is the first collaborative project between L. E. Hewitt and Suzanne Purewal.

Both authors love to hear from their readers!

If you enjoyed this book, please leave a review online at Amazon, Barnes and Noble, or Goodreads!

Check out the latest news and events on L. E. Hewitt's website: www.lehewitt.com

Check out the latest news and events on Suzanne Purewal's website: www.suzannepurewal.com

9 780982 904862